Commotion in the Ocean

To Nicholas & Jonah
G.A.

Extra big thanks to Mandy & Jemima
love from David

Other books by Giles Andreae
and David Wojtowycz

Rumble in the Jungle
The Lion Who Wanted To Love

ISBN 0-439-08214-5

Text copyright © 1998 by Giles Andreae.
Illustrations copyright © 1998 by David Wojtowycz.
All rights reserved.
Published by Scholastic Inc., 555 Broadway, New York, NY 10012,
by arrangement with Little Tiger Press.
Originally published in Great Britain in 1998 by Orchard Books, London.
SCHOLASTIC and associated logos are trademarks and/or registered
trademarks of Scholastic Inc.

12 11 10 9 8 7 6 5 4 3 2   9/9 0 1 2 3 4/0

Printed in the U.S.A.   08

First Scholastic printing, April 1999

Commotion in the Ocean

Giles Andreae

Illustrated by

David Wojtowycz

SCHOLASTIC INC.

New York Toronto London Auckland Sydney
Mexico City New Delhi Hong Kong

Commotion in the Ocean

There's a curious commotion
At the bottom of the ocean.
I think we ought to go and take a look.

You'll find every sort of creature
That lives beneath the sea
Swimming through the pages of this book.

There are dolphins, whales, and penguins,
There are jellyfish and sharks,
There's the turtle and the big white polar bear.

But can you see behind the wrecks
And in between the rocks?
Let's take a look and find who's hiding there. . . .

Crab

The crab likes walking sideways
And I think the reason why
Is to make himself look sneaky
And pretend that he's a spy.

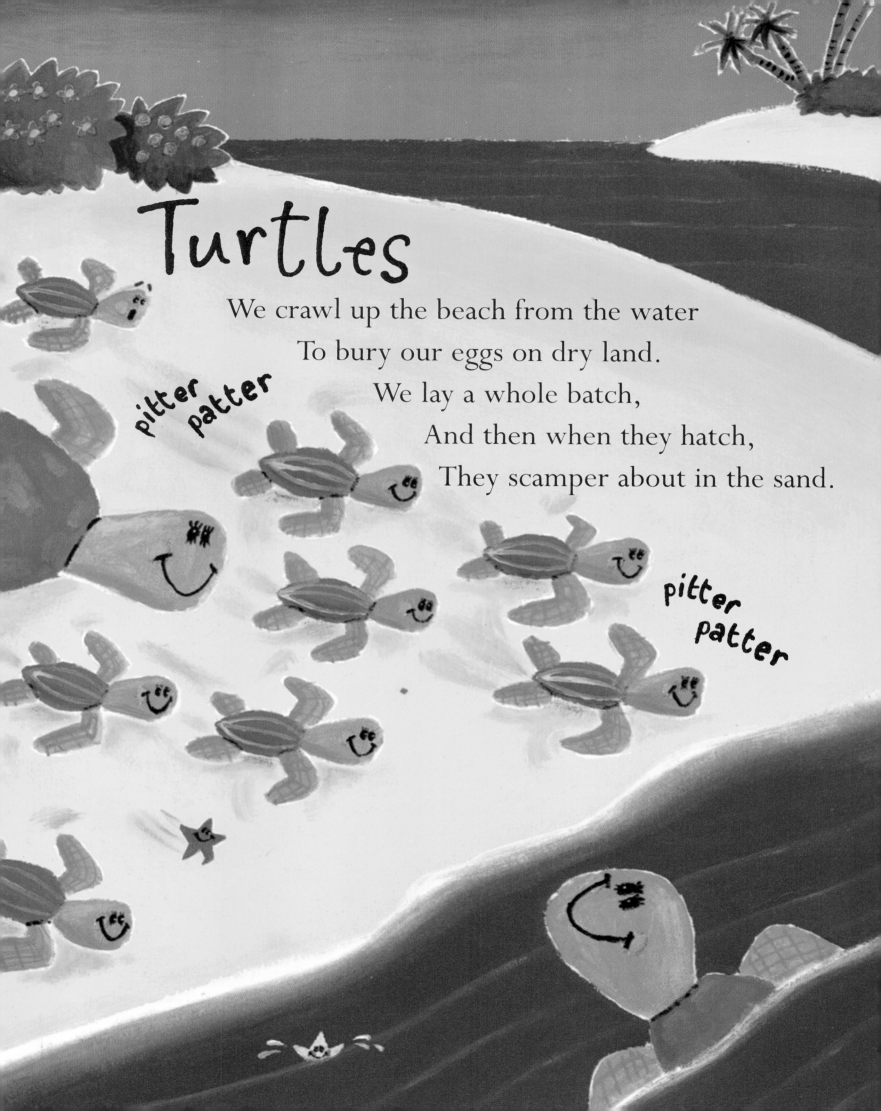

Turtles

We crawl up the beach from the water
To bury our eggs on dry land.
We lay a whole batch,
And then when they hatch,
They scamper about in the sand.

pitter patter

pitter patter

squeak
squeak

click click

Dolphins

The wonderful thing about dolphins
Is hearing them trying to speak.
It's not "How do you do?"
As I'd say to you.
It's more of a "Click-whistle-squeak!"

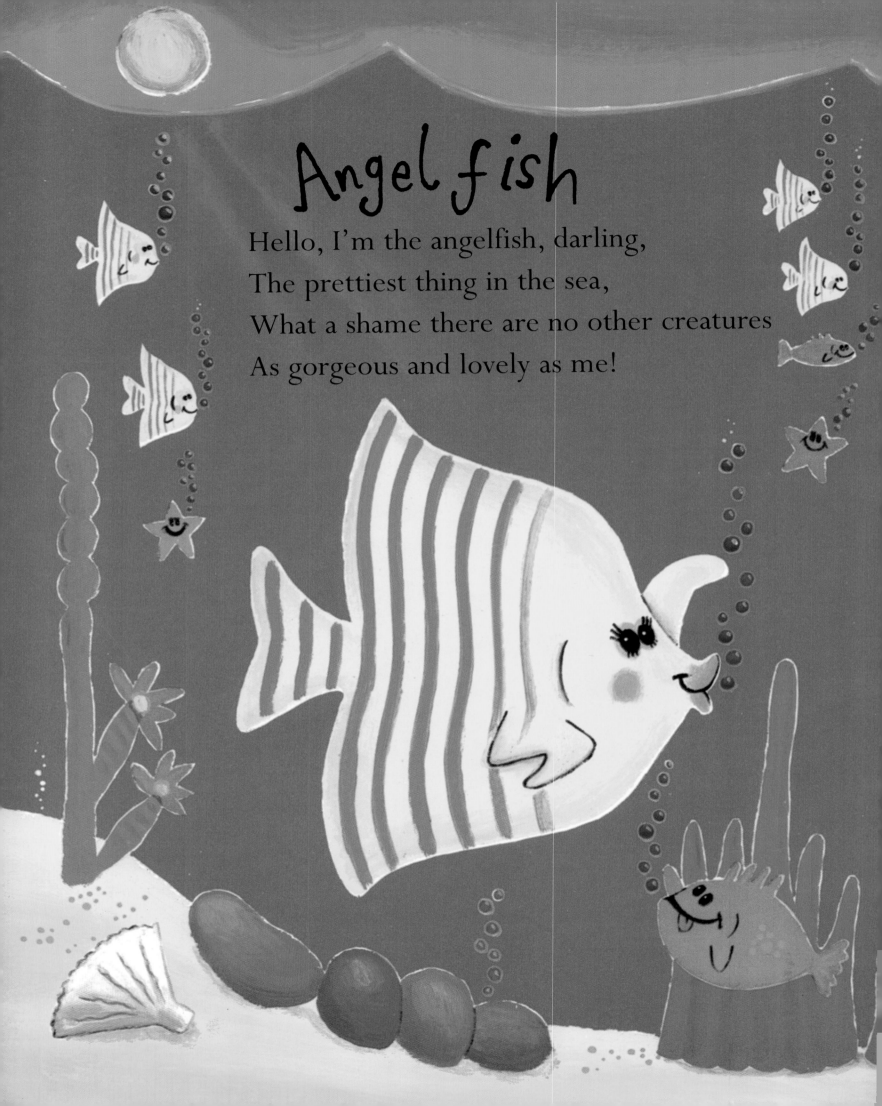

Angelfish

Hello, I'm the angelfish, darling,
The prettiest thing in the sea,
What a shame there are no other creatures
As gorgeous and lovely as me!

Jellyfish

The jellyfish just loves to jiggle
Which other fish think is quite dumb.
She knows that it's not all that useful
But jiggling's lots of good fun.

Shark

I swim with a grin up to greet you,
See how my jaws open wide.
Why don't you come a bit closer?
Please, take a good look inside. . . .

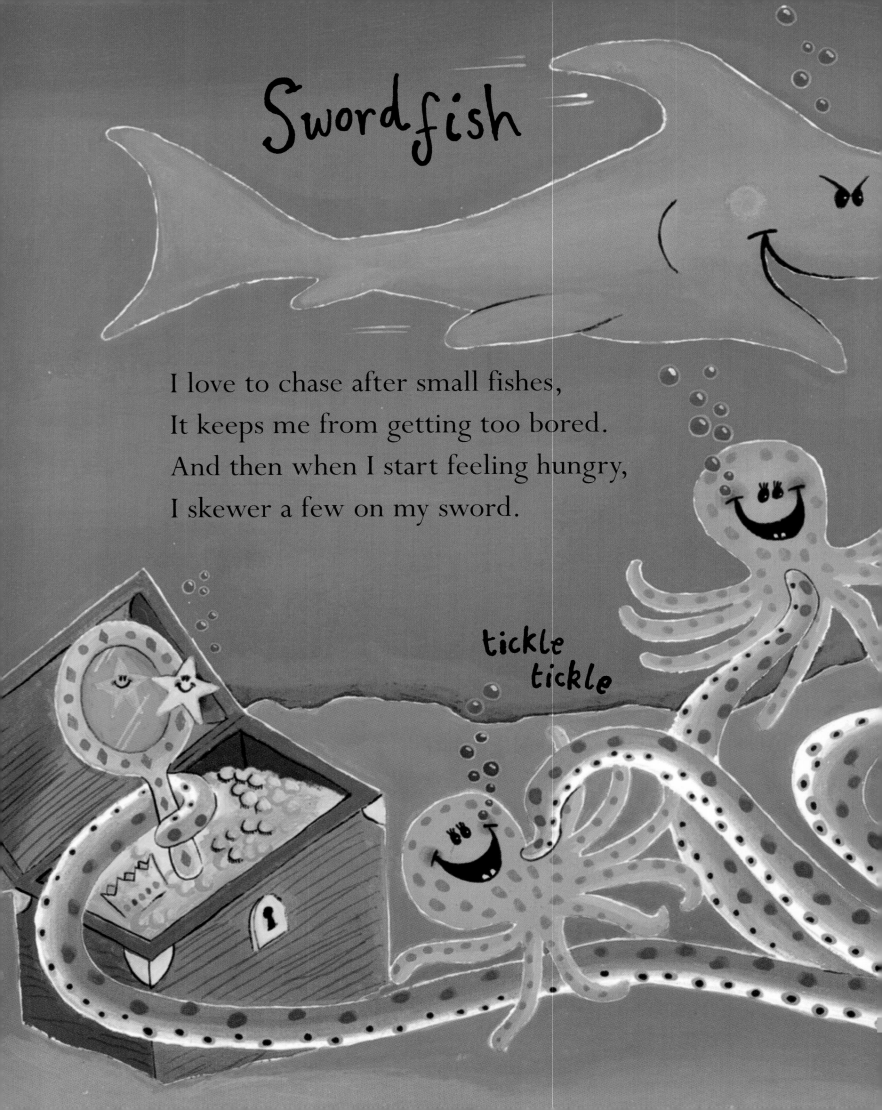

Swordfish

I love to chase after small fishes,
It keeps me from getting too bored.
And then when I start feeling hungry,
I skewer a few on my sword.

tickle
tickle

Octopus

Having eight arms can be useful,
You may think it looks a bit funny,
But it helps me to hold all my children
And tickle each one on the tummy.

tee
hee!

Stingray

At the bottom of the ocean
The stingray flaps his wings.
But don't you get too close to him,
His tail really stings!

Lobster

Never shake hands with a lobster.

It isn't a wise thing to do.

With a clippety-clap

And a snippety-snap,

He would snip all your fingers in two.

Deep Sea

Miles below the surface
Where the water's dark and deep,
Live the most amazing creatures
That you could ever meet.

There are fish of all descriptions,
Of every shape and size.
Some have giant pointy teeth
And great big bulging eyes.

Some of them can walk around
And balance on their fins.
But the strangest fish of all
Have glowing whiskers on their chins!

Blue Whale

There's no other beast on the planet
As big as the giant blue whale.
He measures a massive one hundred feet long
From his head to the tip of his tail.

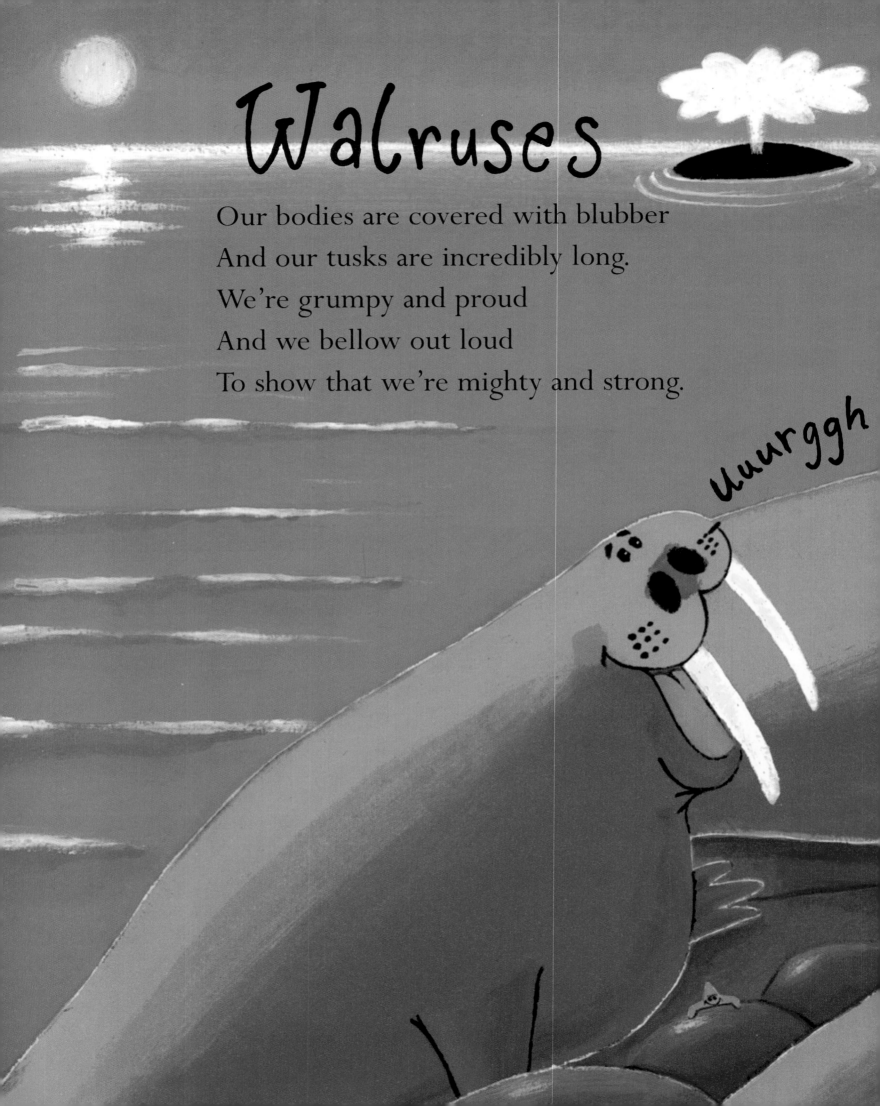

Walruses

Our bodies are covered with blubber
And our tusks are incredibly long.
We're grumpy and proud
And we bellow out loud
To show that we're mighty and strong.

Uuurggh

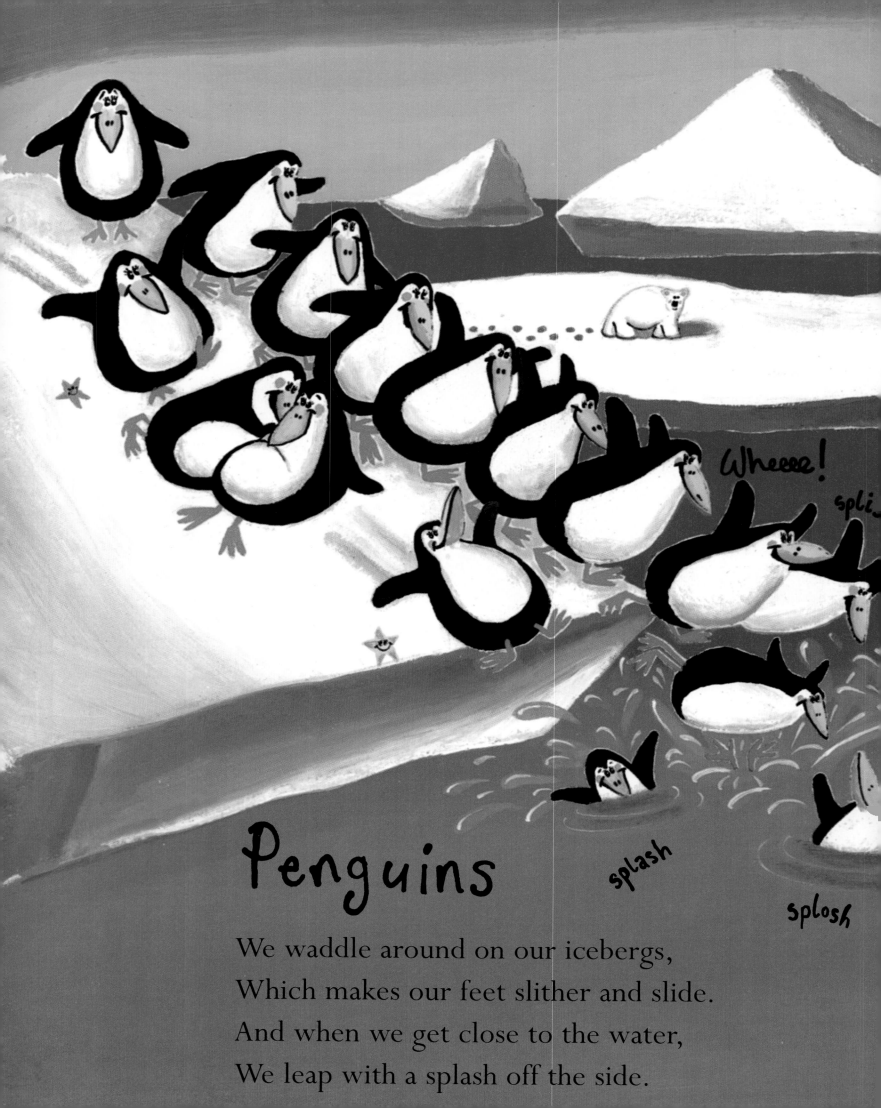

Penguins

We waddle around on our icebergs,
Which makes our feet slither and slide.
And when we get close to the water,
We leap with a splash off the side.

Polar Bears

Deep out in the Arctic

The mommy polar bear

Snuggles up with all her children

Since it's very cold out there.

What a lot of creatures
We have seen beneath the sea,
What a lot of funny things they do.

Some of them might lick their lips
And eat you in one bite,
And some might want to swim around with you.

The dolphin's very friendly
And the lobster's very fierce,
But the shark is the most dangerous by far.

Can you name the other friends
We've made along the way?
See if you can tell me who they are.